THE *Book*
FAMILY ROBINSON

D0183336

MATT CHEZ

How To Start A Fire

DESERT ISLAND SUPERFOODS

COCO NUTZ

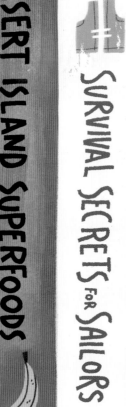

SURVIVAL SECRETS FOR SAILORS

LEE KEELBOAT

BUILD YOUR OWN TREE HOUSE

HOMER BUVGROUND

ISLAND ADVENTURE
ARCHIE PELAGO

FUNNY MONKEY GOES TO THE TOILET

A.P. Shenanigans

HOW TO RUN A LIBRARY

LEN DINGBOOKS

NAVIGATING THE OCEAN

MILES FROMLAND

Cooking Casseroles

STU POTTS

DISCOVERING Long Lost TREASURE

YOUR FORTUNE

For The Book Family Toft - J E

For Jane & Stephen - S C

A TEMPLAR BOOK

First published in the UK in 2022 by Templar Books,
an imprint of Bonnier Books UK
4th Floor, Victoria House
Bloomsbury Square, London WC1B 4DA
Owned by Bonnier Books
Sveavägen 56, Stockholm, Sweden
www.bonnierbooks.co.uk

Text copyright © 2022 by Jonathan Emmett
Illustrations copyright © 2022 by Sam Caldwell

13 5 7 9 10 8 6 4 2

All rights reserved

ISBN 978-1-80078-131-3 (Paperback)

This title was set in Mr Eaves and GStantonICG.
The illustrations were created using graphite, gouache and digital.

Designed by Verity Clark
Edited by Alison Ritchie

Printed in China

MIX
Paper from
responsible sources
FSC® C104723
FSC
www.fsc.org

THE Book
FAMILY ROBINSON

Jonathan Emmett   Sam Caldwell

templar
books

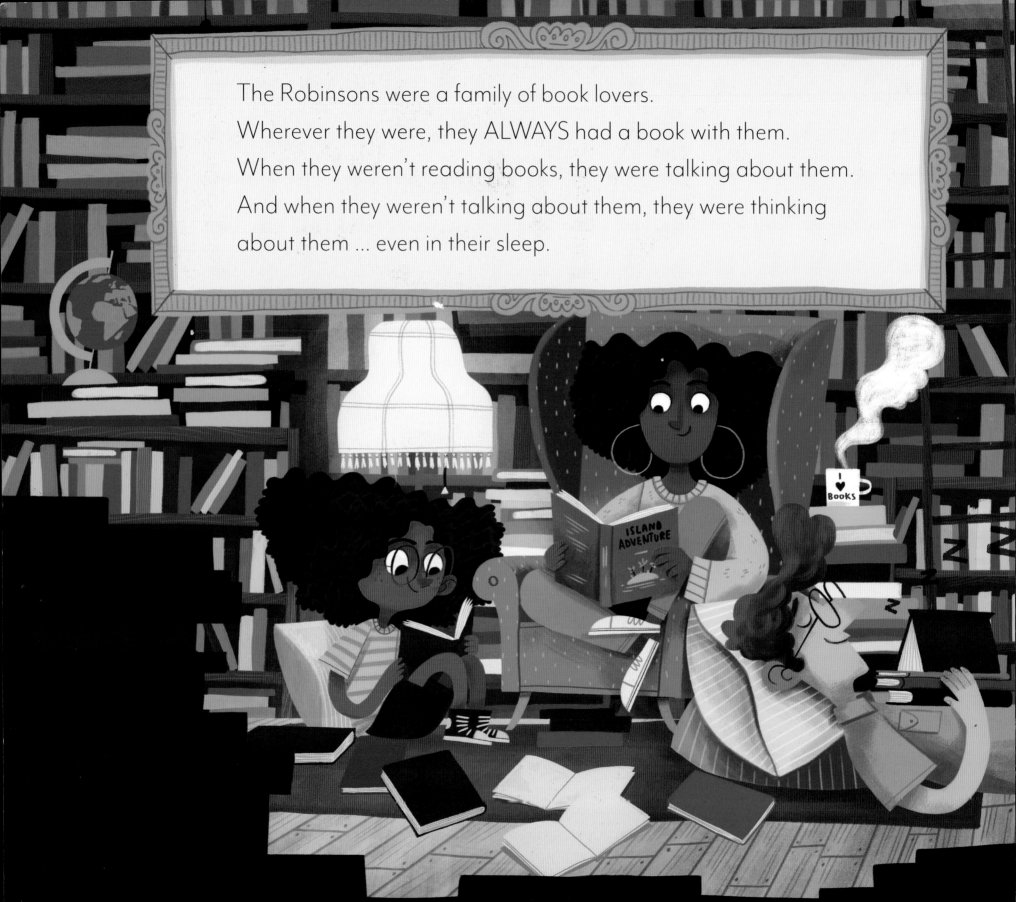

The Robinsons were a family of book lovers.

Wherever they were, they ALWAYS had a book with them.

When they weren't reading books, they were talking about them.

And when they weren't talking about them, they were thinking

about them ... even in their sleep.

The Robinsons read books about all sorts of things. Except for baby Charlie, who wanted to read the same board book, *Funny Monkey Goes to the Toilet*, again and again.

"Poop! Poop!" giggled Charlie, pointing at his favourite page.

One summer the Robinsons decided to go on a sailing holiday.

They obviously wanted to take a few books with them, but which ones?

It was easy for Charlie to choose...

... but not so easy for the rest of the family.

So in the end, they took THE LOT!

They loaded the books onto
a sailing boat and set off,
out into the middle
of the ocean.

And everything was going wonderfully until ...

... THE STORM!

"All hands on deck!" shouted Emily, as a bolt of lightning split the sky.

"Batten down the hatches!" shouted Mr Robinson, as a huge wave crashed over them.

EXCITING STORIES
CLIFF HANGER

SURVIVAL SKILLS FOR SAILORS
LEE KEELBOAT

NAVIGATING THE OCEAN
MILES FROMLAND

DESERT ISLAND SURP...
COCO NUTZ

The next morning the Robinsons found themselves – and all of their books – washed up on the shore of a desert island.

CHAPTER 1

Feeling lucky to be alive, they began – with the help of a few good books –
to make themselves at home.

Mrs Robinson built a new home by following the instructions in *Build Your Own Tree House.*

Mr Robinson found something to eat using *Desert Island Superfoods.*

How to Start a Fire showed Emily how to keep everyone warm.

And Charlie's favourite book inspired him and Juno to dig a toilet of their own.

Poop! Poop!

As they finished digging the hole, they discovered something buried in the ground. It was a huge hoard of TREASURE!

"Well this will brighten the place up," said Mr Robinson.

"But who left it here?" wondered Emily.

A month went by without any sign of rescue. But with a roof over their heads, food to eat and plenty of books to read, the Robinsons lived happily on the island.

Then one day, Emily spotted something on the horizon. It was a pirate ship called *The Evil Weevil*. And it was sailing their way!

The pirates had come to collect a hoard of treasure they'd hidden on the island.

But when they got to the spot where they'd buried the treasure ...

... they found that the Robinsons had dug it all up!

The pirates were **VERY ANGRY**. And their Captain, Betsy Bloodbucket, was the angriest of them all.

"What do we do with land-lubbers who takes our treasure?" she snarled.

"You let them give it back and forgive them?" suggested Mr Robinson, hopefully.

"WE MAKES 'EM WALK THE PLANK!" shouted the crew.

The pirates tied the Robinsons up, took them back to *The Evil Weevil* and forced them out onto the plank.

"Any last words before yer meets yer doom?" growled Captain Bloodbucket.

The Robinsons were too scared to say anything – except Charlie.

"**Poop! Poop!**" said Charlie, waving his favourite book under the Captain's nose.

As fierce as Captain Bloodbucket was, she couldn't refuse Charlie his final request. So she sat him on her knee and read *Funny Monkey Goes to the Toilet.*

By the time she'd finished, the Captain was roaring with laughter. She thought *Funny Monkey Goes to the Toilet* was THE most rib-ticklingly hilarious thing she'd ever seen. And the crew were all laughing too.

"Can we have another book?" asked the first mate eagerly.

"We've got plenty more," said Emily.

"And we'd be very happy to share them with you," said Mrs Robinson.

"Shiver me timbers!" said Captain Bloodbucket, when she saw the Robinsons' huge book collection back on the island. "What a treasure trove!"

With a little help from the Robinsons, every pirate found a book they enjoyed reading ...

... or having read to them!

And the hungry sea monster reached out a huge slimy tentacle and ...

And, after a few days, the pirates realised that they were much happier reading books than raiding ships. So they sold their hoard of treasure and used the money to convert *The Evil Weevil* pirate ship into ...

The Funny Monkey Floating Library!

HISPANOLA

The pirates and the Robinsons sailed the ocean together,
lending books to all the ships and islands that they came across.

A good library needs good librarians and
The Funny Monkey Floating Library
had the very best.

THE
FUNNY MONKEY
FLOATING LIBRARY

THE UNICORN

The Robinsons were a family of book lovers.
Wherever they were, they always had a book with them.
And these days, they always have a SHIPFUL!

MATT CHEZ — *How To Start A Fire*

DESERT ISLAND SUPERFOODS — COCO NUTZ

SURVIVAL SECRETS FOR SAILORS — LEE KEERBOAT

BUILD YOUR OWN TREE HOUSE — HOMER BUVGROUND

ISLAND ADVENTURE
ARCHIE PELAGO

FUNNY MONKEY GOES TO THE TOILET
A.P. Shenanigans

HOW TO RUN A LIBRARY
LEN DINGBOOKS

NAVIGATING THE OCEAN
MILES FROMLAND

Cooking Casseroles
STU POTTS

DISCOVERING LONG LOST TREASURE
IVOR FORTUNE